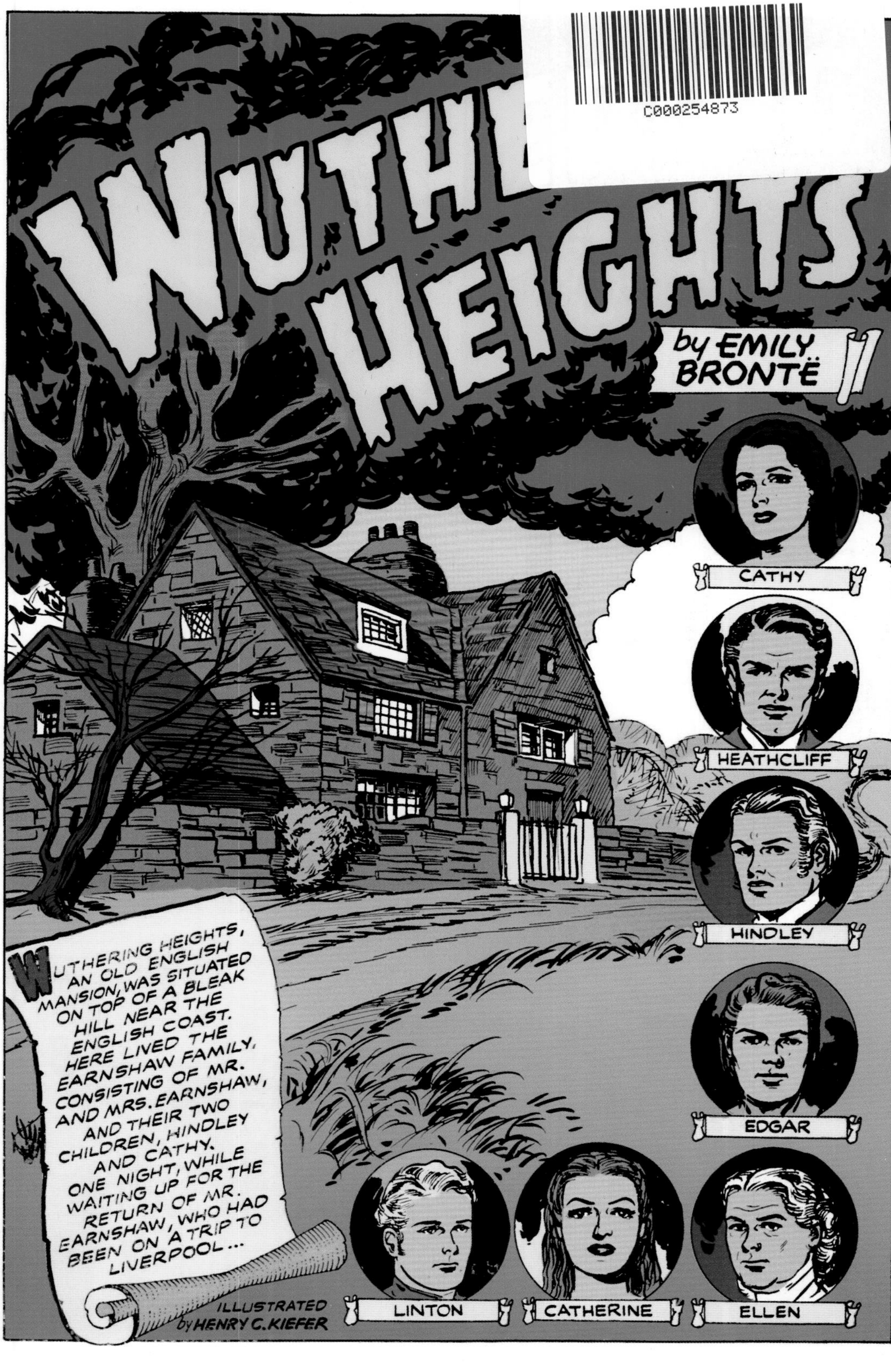
WUTHERING HEIGHTS
by EMILY BRONTË
CATHY
HEATHCLIFF
HINDLEY
EDGAR
WUTHERING HEIGHTS, AN OLD ENGLISH MANSION, WAS SITUATED ON TOP OF A BLEAK HILL NEAR THE ENGLISH COAST. HERE LIVED THE EARNSHAW FAMILY, CONSISTING OF MR. AND MRS. EARNSHAW, AND THEIR TWO CHILDREN, HINDLEY AND CATHY. ONE NIGHT, WHILE WAITING UP FOR THE RETURN OF MR. EARNSHAW, WHO HAD BEEN ON A TRIP TO LIVERPOOL...
ILLUSTRATED by HENRY C. KIEFER
LINTON
CATHERINE
ELLEN

LOOK, WIFE, WHAT I BROUGHT HOME!

BUT WHAT... WHO IS IT?

I FOUND HIM ON THE STREETS OF LIVERPOOL, STARVING AND HOMELESS. NOT A SOUL KNEW TO WHOM HE BELONGED, SO I'VE BROUGHT HIM HOME.

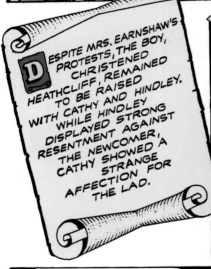

DESPITE MRS. EARNSHAW'S PROTESTS, THE BOY, CHRISTENED HEATHCLIFF, REMAINED TO BE RAISED WITH CATHY AND HINDLEY. WHILE HINDLEY DISPLAYED STRONG RESENTMENT AGAINST THE NEWCOMER, CATHY SHOWED A STRANGE AFFECTION FOR THE LAD.

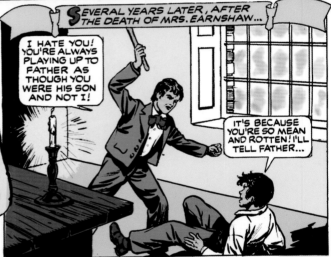

SEVERAL YEARS LATER, AFTER THE DEATH OF MRS. EARNSHAW...

I HATE YOU! YOU'RE ALWAYS PLAYING UP TO FATHER AS THOUGH YOU WERE HIS SON AND NOT I!

IT'S BECAUSE YOU'RE SO MEAN AND ROTTEN! I'LL TELL FATHER...

HINDLEY! HOW MANY TIMES HAVE I TOLD YOU NOT TO MISTREAT YOUR BROTHER? LET ME CATCH YOU ONCE MORE AND I'LL GIVE YOU THE HIDING OF YOUR LIFE!

HE'S NOT MY BROTHER! HE'S A FILTHY...

SILENCE, HINDLEY! GO OUT TO THE STABLE, YOU TWO, AND SEE WHAT I BROUGHT HOME FROM THE PARISH FAIR!

AT THE STABLE, THE BOYS FOUND TWO COLTS. HEATHCLIFF IMMEDIATELY CHOSE THE HANDSOMER. LATER, HIS HORSE WENT LAME...

NOW, YOUR HORSE IS LAME AND IT SERVES YOU RIGHT!

YOU MUST EXCHANGE HORSES WITH ME, HINDLEY; AND IF YOU WON'T, I SHALL TELL FATHER OF THE THRASHINGS YOU'VE GIVEN ME THIS WEEK!

WHY, YOU LOW-DOWN DIRTY CUR! JUST LET ME GET MY HANDS ON YOU!

HEATHCLIFF ESCAPED TO THE PORCH, BUT PERSISTED...

YOU'D BETTER DO IT AT ONCE! OR I'LL SPEAK TO FATHER OF THESE BLOWS AND YOU'LL GET THEM BACK WITH INTEREST!

OFF, DOG!

THROW IT, AND THEN I'LL TELL HOW YOU BOASTED THAT YOU WOULD TURN ME OUT OF DOORS AS SOON AS FATHER DIED, AND SEE WHETHER HE WILL NOT TURN YOU OUT DIRECTLY!

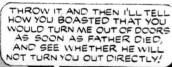

TAKING HIM AT HIS WORD, HINDLEY HEAVED THE WEIGHT, STRIKING HEATHCLIFF IN THE CHEST...

ELLEN DEAN, THE HOUSEKEEPER, CAME TO THE RESCUE...

I'LL GO TO THE MASTER AND TELL HIM HINDLEY TRIED TO KILL ME!

NO, HEATHCLIFF, YOU MUSTN'T! THAT WOULD ONLY MAKE THINGS WORSE!

LATER, FEARFUL THAT HEATHCLIFF WOULD TELL HIS FATHER OF THE INCIDENT, HINDLEY IS FORCED TO GIVE IN...

TAKE MY COLT, GYPSY! AND I PRAY THAT HE MAY BREAK YOUR NECK!

HINDLEY THEN SENT HEATHCLIFF SPRAWLING UNDER THE COLT'S FEET...

TAKE THAT! AND I HOPE HE KICKS YOUR BRAINS OUT!

WITHOUT A WORD, HEATHCLIFF COOLY PICKED HIMSELF UP AND LED THE BEAST AWAY, SATISFIED THAT HE HAD GOTTEN WHAT HE WANTED...

IN THE COURSE OF TIME, MR. EARNSHAW'S HEALTH BEGAN TO FAIL, AND HE BECAME MORE IRRITABLE WITH HINDLEY...

I TELL YOU, CURATE, THAT BOY WILL BE THE DEATH OF ME.

FOR YOUR OWN PEACE, I WOULD ADVISE SENDING HINDLEY OFF TO COLLEGE.

HINDLEY WAS SENT OFF TO COLLEGE, AND FOR A WHILE, IT LOOKED LIKE THERE WOULD BE SOME PEACE IN THE HOUSEHOLD...

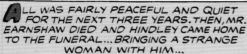

ALL WAS FAIRLY PEACEFUL AND QUIET FOR THE NEXT THREE YEARS. THEN, MR. EARNSHAW DIED AND HINDLEY CAME HOME TO THE FUNERAL...BRINGING A STRANGE WOMAN WITH HIM...

NELLY, MEET MY WIFE...WE'VE COME HOME TO STAY.

WIFE! WELL, WELCOME TO WUTHERING HEIGHTS.

YOU MUST WASH UP, MY DEAR, AND I'LL FIX UP A ROOM FOR YOU AND HINDLEY.

HINDLEY WAS NOW MASTER...

YOU AND JOSEPH MUST HENCEFORTH CONFINE YOURSELVES TO THE BACK KITCHEN AND LEAVE THE HOUSE TO ME!

AS FOR YOU, HEATHCLIFF, YOU'LL LIVE WITH THE SERVANTS AND WILL RECEIVE NO INSTRUCTIONS FROM THE CURATE!

IT IS MY WISH THAT YOU SPEND YOUR TIME OUTDOORS LABOURING WITH THE OTHER HELP ON THE FARM. I SHALL BE THE MASTER OF WUTHERING HEIGHTS!

HEATHCLIFF BORE HIS DEGRADATION WELL. CATHY TAUGHT HIM WHAT SHE LEARNED AND WORKED OR PLAYED WITH HIM IN THE FIELDS...

IT WAS ONE OF THE CHIEF AMUSEMENTS OF THE TWO TO RUN AWAY TO THE MOORS IN THE MORNING AND REMAIN THERE ALL DAY. ONE SUNDAY EVENING...

THRUSHCROSS GRANGE IS ALL LIT UP TONIGHT! LET'S GO AND SEE HOW THE LINTONS LIVE.

I SUPPOSE THE CHILDREN PASS THEIR SUNDAY EVENINGS SHIVERING IN CORNERS.

YES, AND IF IT'S ANYTHING LIKE OUR HOUSE, THEIR FATHER AND MOTHER ARE PROBABLY AT THEIR MEAL, SINGING AND LAUGHING AND BURNING THEIR EYES OUT BEFORE THE FIRE.

THEY MADE THEIR WAY THROUGH A BROKEN HEDGE, GROPED THEIR WAY UP THE PATH AND PEERED INTO THE DRAWING-ROOM WINDOW...

WHAT MET THEIR EYES WAS A PETTY QUARREL AMIDST A SCENE OF SPLENDOR...

THE DOG IS MINE... PAPA GAVE IT TO ME!

HE DID NOT! HE GAVE IT TO BOTH OF US!

IMAGINE THEM QUARRELING OVER A HEAP OF WARM HAIR!

YOU'D THINK THEY'D BE HAPPY LIVING IN SUCH A LOVELY HOUSE, WITH ALL THOSE PRETTY CLOTHES AND EVERYTHING!

HEARING THE INTRUDERS OUTSIDE THE WINDOW...

THERE'S SOMEBODY OUTSIDE THE WINDOW!

OH, MAMA, MAMA! OH! PAPA...COME HERE, QUICK!

AS CATHY AND HEATHCLIFF STARTED TO RUN AWAY, THEY WERE ATTACKED BY A SAVAGE DOG.

RUN, HEATHCLIFF, RUN! BEFORE THE DOG GETS YOU, TOO!

LET GO, YOU CURSED BEAST!

KEEP FAST, SKULKER! KEEP... GOOD HEAVENS, IT'S A LITTLE GIRL!

THE DOG WAS BEATEN OFF AND THE SERVANT CARRIED CATHY INTO THE HOUSE...

WHAT PREY, ROBERT?

SKULKER HAS CAUGHT A LITTLE GIRL, SIR.. AND THERE'S A LAD HERE, TOO!

LOOK AT THAT RAGGED-LOOKING BOY! ISN'T HE THE FRIGHTFUL THING?

EDGAR WHISPERED TO HIS MOTHER...

THAT'S MISS EARNSHAW, MOTHER. I'M SURE I'VE SEEN HER AT CHURCH!

NONSENSE! AND YET, SHE IS IN MOURNING...

HE MUST BE THAT STRANGE ACQUISITION MY LATE NEIGHBOUR MADE, IN HIS JOURNEY TO LIVERPOOL.

A WICKED BOY AT ALL EVENTS AND QUITE UNFIT FOR A DECENT HOUSE. TELL ROBERT TO TAKE HIM OFF... WE'LL TAKE CARE OF THE INJURED GIRL!

LATE THAT NIGHT, HEATHCLIFF RETURNED ALONE TO WUTHERING HEIGHTS, AND TOLD HIS STORY TO ELLEN...

THERE WILL MORE COME OF THIS THAN YOU RECKON. YOU ARE INCURABLE, HEATHCLIFF... MR. HINDLEY WILL ORDER ANOTHER FLOGGING FOR YOU, SEE IF HE WON'T!

CATHY STAYED FIVE WEEKS AT THRUSHCROSS GRANGE.. UNTIL CHRISTMAS. HINDLEY'S WIFE VISITED HER OFTEN IN THE INTERVAL, AND IN AN ATTEMPT TO RAISE CATHY'S RESPECT, SHOWERED HER WITH FINE CLOTHES AND FLATTERY, WHICH THE GIRL TOOK READILY...

CATHY ARRIVED AT WUTHERING HEIGHTS RICHLY ATTIRED, QUITE UNLIKE THE WILD, HATLESS LITTLE SAVAGE THAT HAD LEFT SOME WEEKS BEFORE...

WHY, CATHY, YOU'RE QUITE A BEAUTY! SHE LOOKS LIKE A LADY NOW, DOESN'T SHE, FRANCES?

YES, BUT SHE MUST MIND AND NOT GROW WILD AGAIN HERE.

WHY, CATHY, I HARDLY RECOGNISED YOU!

IS HEATHCLIFF NOT HERE?

HEATHCLIFF, COME FORWARD! YOU MAY COME AND WISH MISS CATHERINE WELCOME, LIKE THE OTHER SERVANTS!

CATCHING A GLIMPSE OF HER FRIEND, CATHY FLEW TO EMBRACE HIM...

WHY, HOW VERY BLACK AND CROSS YOU LOOK...AND HOW...HOW FUNNY AND GRIM. BUT THAT'S BECAUSE I'M USED TO EDGAR AND ISABELLA LINTON. WELL, HEATHCLIFF, HAVE YOU FORGOTTEN ME?

SHAKE HANDS, HEATHCLIFF...ONCE, IN A WAY THAT IS PERMITTED!

I SHALL NOT! I SHALL NOT STAND TO BE LAUGHED AT...I SHALL NOT BEAR IT!

I DID NOT MEAN TO LAUGH AT YOU, HEATHCLIFF! IT WAS ONLY THAT YOU LOOKED ODD...AND YOU ARE SO DIRTY!

I SHALL BE DIRTY AS I PLEASE...AND I LIKE TO BE DIRTY!

WITH THAT, HE DASHED OUT OF THE ROOM, AMID THE MERRIMENT OF THE MASTER AND MISTRESS AND TO THE SERIOUS DISTURBANCE OF CATHY...

CHRISTMAS EVE CAME. THE EARNSHAWS MADE PREPARATIONS TO RECEIVE EDGAR AND ISABELLA LINTON, WHO HAD BEEN INVITED FOR THE MORROW...

CHRISTMAS MORNING...

NELLY, MAKE ME DECENT WHILE THE OTHERS ARE IN CHURCH!

WELL, IT IS CERTAINLY HIGH TIME, HEATHCLIFF!

THEIR CONVERSATION WAS INTERRUPTED BY A RAMBLING SOUND MOVING UP THE ROAD AND ENTERING THE COURT...

THERE ARE THE LINTONS, NOW! YOU MUST BE ON YOUR BEST BEHAVIOUR AND GREET THEM PLEASANTLY.

AS HEATHCLIFF OPENED THE DOOR LEADING FROM THE KITCHEN...

JOSEPH, KEEP THE FELLOW OUT OF THE PARLOUR...SEND HIM TO THE GARRET TILL DINNER IS OVER. HE'LL BE CRAMMING HIS FINGERS INTO EVERYTHING IF LET ALONE A MINUTE.

NAY, SIR, HE'LL TOUCH NOTHING, NOT HE...AND I SUPPOSE HE MUST HAVE HIS SHARE OF THE DAINTIES AS WELL AS WE.

HE SHALL HAVE HIS SHARE OF MY HANDS! I'LL PULL THOSE ELEGANT LOCKS OF HIS A BIT LONGER!

THEY'RE LONG ENOUGH ALREADY! I WONDER WHY THEY DON'T MAKE HIS HEAD ACHE.

WILD WITH RAGE, HEATHCLIFF SEIZED A TUREEN OF HOT APPLESAUCE AND HURLED IT AT EDGAR, HIS TORMENTOR...

THAT'LL TEACH YOU TO HOLD YOUR TONGUE!

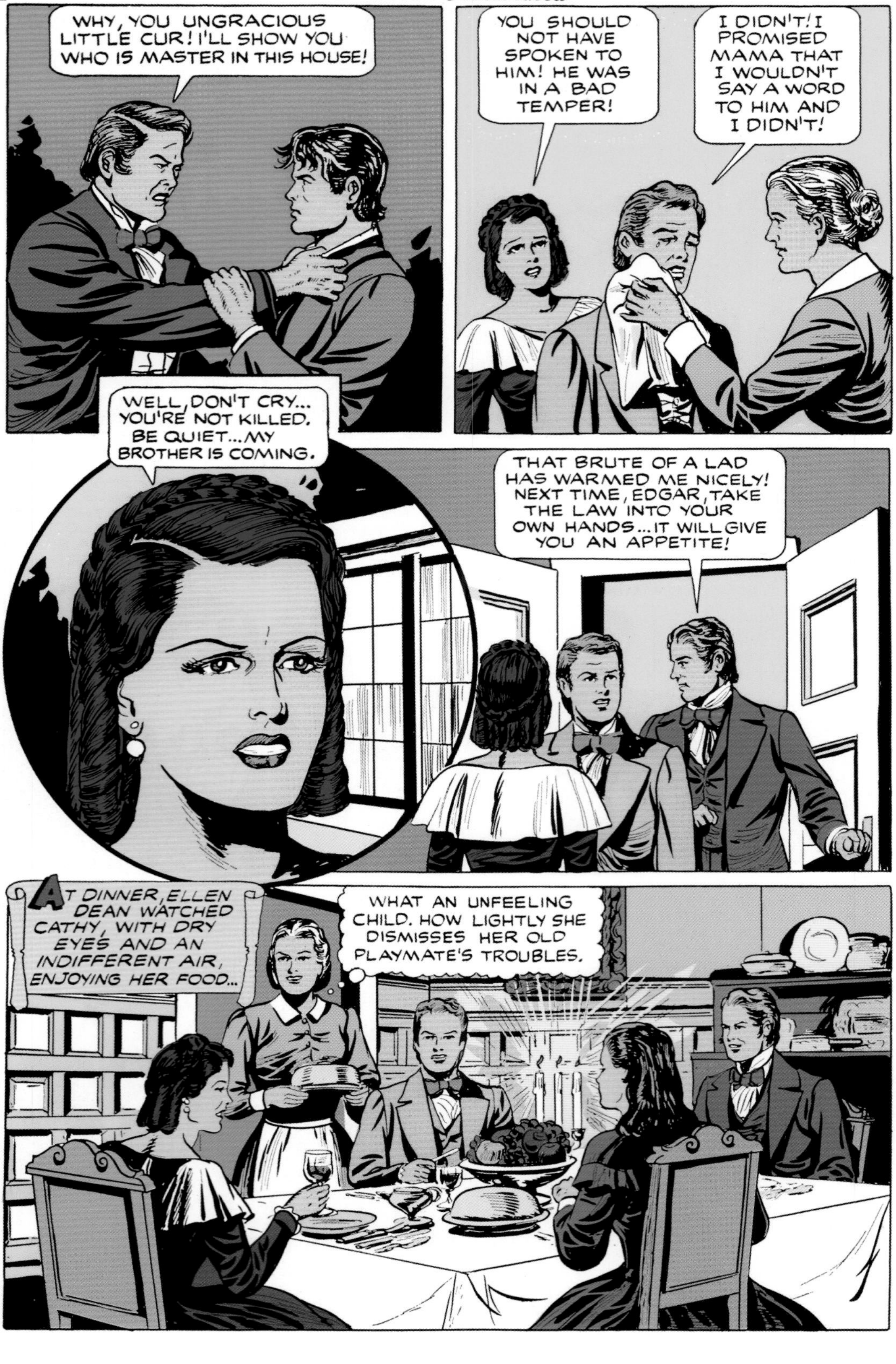
WHY, YOU UNGRACIOUS LITTLE CUR! I'LL SHOW YOU WHO IS MASTER IN THIS HOUSE!
YOU SHOULD NOT HAVE SPOKEN TO HIM! HE WAS IN A BAD TEMPER!
I DIDN'T! I PROMISED MAMA THAT I WOULDN'T SAY A WORD TO HIM AND I DIDN'T!
WELL, DON'T CRY... YOU'RE NOT KILLED. BE QUIET... MY BROTHER IS COMING.
THAT BRUTE OF A LAD HAS WARMED ME NICELY! NEXT TIME, EDGAR, TAKE THE LAW INTO YOUR OWN HANDS... IT WILL GIVE YOU AN APPETITE!
AT DINNER, ELLEN DEAN WATCHED CATHY, WITH DRY EYES AND AN INDIFFERENT AIR, ENJOYING HER FOOD...
WHAT AN UNFEELING CHILD. HOW LIGHTLY SHE DISMISSES HER OLD PLAYMATE'S TROUBLES.

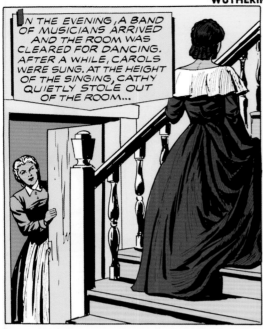

IN THE EVENING, A BAND OF MUSICIANS ARRIVED AND THE ROOM WAS CLEARED FOR DANCING. AFTER A WHILE, CAROLS WERE SUNG. AT THE HEIGHT OF THE SINGING, CATHY QUIETLY STOLE OUT OF THE ROOM...

THERE WAS NO RESPONSE FROM WITHIN...

HEATHCLIFF! PLEASE OPEN UP...I WISH TO SPEAK TO YOU.

ELLEN FOLLOWED HER UP TO THE GARRET WHERE HEATHCLIFF WAS CONFINED...

SHE'S GONE TO HEATHCLIFF'S ROOM. I KNEW SHE COULDN'T FORGET HER FORMER PLAYMATE!

A MOMENT LATER, ELLEN REACHED THE GARRET DOOR...

GOOD HEAVENS, SHE MUST HAVE CLIMBED INTO HIS ROOM THROUGH THE SKYLIGHT.

SOON, THEY CAME OUT OF THE ROOM BY WAY OF THE SKYLIGHT. ELLEN TOOK HEATHCLIFF DOWN TO THE KITCHEN WHILE CATHY WENT BACK TO THE PARTY...

WHAT ARE YOU THINKING ABOUT, HEATHCLIFF?

I'M TRYING TO SETTLE HOW I SHALL PAY HINDLEY BACK.

FOR SHAME! IT IS FOR GOD TO PUNISH WICKED PEOPLE...WE SHOULD LEARN TO FORGIVE.

NO, GOD WON'T HAVE THE SATISFACTION THAT I SHALL!

IN DUE COURSE, A CHILD WAS BORN TO THE EARNSHAWS, BUT THE MOTHER DIED SOON AFTER. OVERCOME BY HIS GRIEF, HINDLEY GAVE HIMSELF UP TO RECKLESS DISSIPATION...

THE CHILD, HARETON, BECAME THE PARTICULAR CHARGE OF ELLEN DEAN...

IT LOOKS LIKE I'LL HAVE TO BE MOTHER AND FATHER TO YOU FROM NOW ON, MY LITTLE SWEET!

SOMETIME LATER, WHILE HINDLEY WAS AWAY FROM THE HEIGHTS...

CATHY, ARE YOU BUSY THIS AFTERNOON? ARE YOU GOING OUT?

NO, IT IS RAINING, HEATHCLIFF.

WHY HAVE YOU THAT SILK FROCK ON, THEN? NOBODY COMING HERE, I HOPE!

NOT THAT I KNOW OF... BUT YOU SHOULD BE IN THE FIELD NOW, HEATHCLIFF. IT IS AN HOUR PAST DINNER-TIME ...YOU SHOULD BE GONE!

HINDLEY DOES NOT OFTEN FREE US FROM HIS ACCURSED PRESENCE! I'LL NOT WORK ANY MORE...I'LL STAY WITH YOU! YOU'VE BEEN MORE WITH THE LINTONS THAN WITH ME!

"THEIR CONVERSATION WAS INTERRUPTED BY THE SOUND OF A HORSE'S HOOFS IN THE COURT...

EDGAR LINTON SOON CAME IN AND CATHY MARKED THE DIFFERENCE BETWEEN HER FRIENDS...AS ONE CAME IN, AND THE OTHER LEFT...

SO SHE WAS EXPECTING COMPANY!

I'M NOT COME TOO SOON, AM I?

NO. WHAT ARE YOU DOING THERE, NELLY?

HINDLEY HAD GIVEN ELLEN INSTRUCTIONS TO BE PRESENT AT ANY PRIVATE VISITS OF EDGAR LINTON...

MY WORK, MISS!

SHE STEPPED BEHIND ELLEN AND WHISPERED CROSSLY...

TAKE YOURSELF AND YOUR DUSTER OFF! WHEN COMPANY IS IN THE HOUSE, SERVANTS DON'T COMMENCE CLEANING IN THE ROOM WHERE THEY ARE!

I'M SURE MR. LINTON WILL EXCUSE ME!

IRRESISTIBLY IMPELLED BY THE MEAN SPIRIT WITHIN HER, CATHY SLAPPED HER ON THE CHEEK...

CATHERINE, LOVE! CATHERINE!

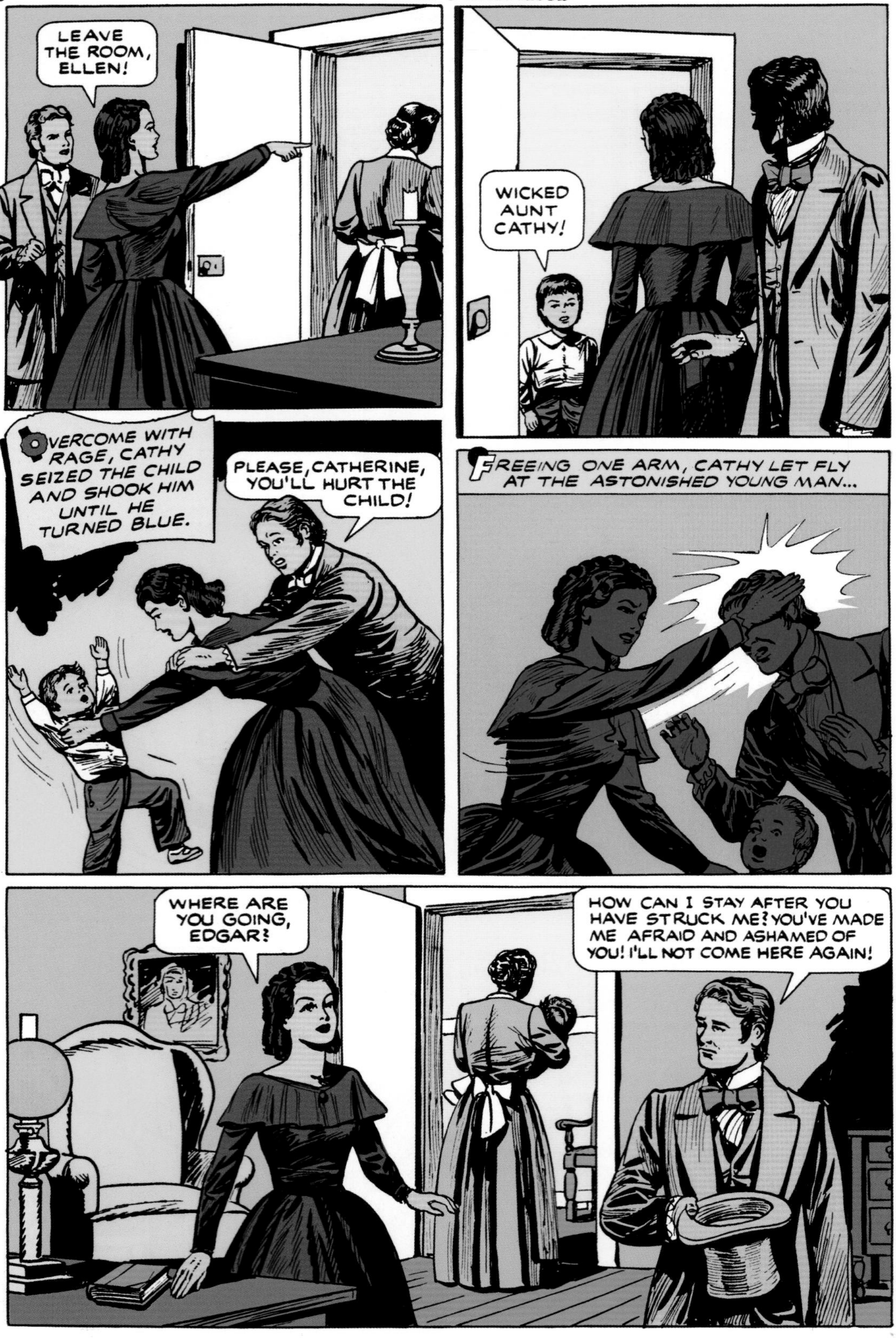
LEAVE THE ROOM, ELLEN!
WICKED AUNT CATHY!
OVERCOME WITH RAGE, CATHY SEIZED THE CHILD AND SHOOK HIM UNTIL HE TURNED BLUE.
PLEASE, CATHERINE, YOU'LL HURT THE CHILD!
FREEING ONE ARM, CATHY LET FLY AT THE ASTONISHED YOUNG MAN...
WHERE ARE YOU GOING, EDGAR?
HOW CAN I STAY AFTER YOU HAVE STRUCK ME? YOU'VE MADE ME AFRAID AND ASHAMED OF YOU! I'LL NOT COME HERE AGAIN!

CATHY DROPPED DOWN ON HER KNEES AND SET TO WEEPING IN EARNEST...

OVERCOME BY CATHY'S DISPLAY OF SELF-PITY, EDGAR REMAINED TO COMFORT HER...

YOU DON'T CARE ABOUT ME! WHY DON'T YOU GO?

PLEASE, CATHERINE, I CAN'T BEAR TO SEE YOU CRY! I LOVE YOU, DARLING!

ELLEN APPEARED SUDDENLY...

YOU'D BETTER GO NOW, MASTER EDGAR! HINDLEY'S COME HOME AND HE'S DRUNK!

EDGAR RAN SPEEDILY TO HIS HORSE AND CATHY TO HER CHAMBER. ELLEN WENT TO HIDE LITTLE HARETON AND REMOVE THE SHOT FROM HINDLEY'S FOWLING PIECE *

* OLD TIME RIFLE

THERE, I'VE FOUND YOU AT LAST! WITH THE HELP OF SATAN, I SHALL MAKE YOU SWALLOW A CARVING KNIFE! HIDING MY OWN CHILD FROM ME!

SO YOU'RE AFRAID OF ME, YOUR OWN FATHER! AS SURE AS I'M LIVING, I'LL BREAK THE BRAT'S NECK!

HE CARRIED THE STRUGGLING CHILD UP THE STAIRS AND LIFTED HIM OVER THE BANNISTER...

PLEASE, MASTER HINDLEY, YOU'LL FRIGHTEN THE CHILD INTO FITS!

HINDLEY WAS MOMENTARILY ATTRACTED BY A NOISE FROM BELOW...

WHO IS THAT?

YOU'RE WORSE THAN A HEATHEN!

BY A NATURAL IMPULSE, HEATHCLIFF ARRESTED THE CHILD'S DESCENT...

TAKE THE BRAT OUT OF MY SIGHT! AND YOU, HEATHCLIFF, CLEAR OUT BEFORE I GET AN INCLINATION TO MURDER YOU!

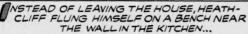

INSTEAD OF LEAVING THE HOUSE, HEATHCLIFF FLUNG HIMSELF ON A BENCH NEAR THE WALL IN THE KITCHEN...

SOME TIME LATER, CATHY, UNAWARE OF HEATHCLIFF'S PRESENCE...

ARE YOU ALONE, NELLY? WHERE'S HEATHCLIFF?

ABOUT HIS WORK IN THE STABLE, I SUPPOSE!

EDGAR LINTON ASKED ME TO MARRY HIM. NOW, BEFORE I TELL YOU WHAT MY ANSWER WAS, YOU TELL ME WHAT IT OUGHT TO HAVE BEEN!

I MUST SAY HE IS HOPELESSLY STUPID OR A VENTURESOME FOOL. WHAT ABOUT HEATHCLIFF?

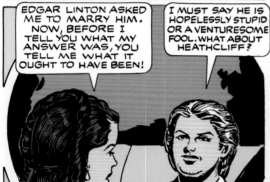

IT WOULD DEGRADE ME TO MARRY HEATHCLIFF NOW...SO HE SHALL NEVER KNOW HOW I LOVE HIM. WHATEVER OUR SOULS ARE MADE OF, THEY'RE THE SAME!

HEATHCLIFF HAD LISTENED TILL HE HEARD CATHY SAY HE WOULD DEGRADE HER, AND THEN STOLE NOISELESSLY OUT...

CATHY, I'VE COME TO THE CONCLUSION THAT YOU ARE A WICKED, UNPRINCIPLED GIRL! IF YOU MARRY EDGAR, YOU'LL REGRET IT AS LONG AS YOU LIVE!

HEATHCLIFF HAD COMPLETELY DISAPPEARED FROM WUTHERING HEIGHTS. SOME TIME LATER, CATHY AND EDGAR LINTON WERE MARRIED...

SOON AFTER THEIR MARRIAGE...

NELLY, I WANT YOU TO COME AND LIVE WITH ME AT THRUSHCROSS GRANGE.

NO, CATHERINE, I MUST STAY HERE WITH HARETON!

WHEN ELLEN REFUSED, CATHY PREVAILED UPON HER HUSBAND AND BROTHER HINDLEY TO PERSUADE HER TO LEAVE WUTHERING HEIGHTS...

I'LL HAVE NO MORE OF THIS, ELLEN! PACK UP AND GO! I WANT NO WOMAN IN THE HOUSE, NOW THAT THERE'S NO MISTRESS. THE CURATE WILL TAKE THE CHILD IN HAND LATER!

I'LL GO, MASTER HINDLEY, BUT I MUST SAY YOU GOT RID OF ALL DECENT PEOPLE ONLY TO RUN TO RUIN A LITTLE FASTER.

ELLEN HAD NO OTHER CHOICE BUT TO OBEY HINDLEY'S ORDERS. AND SO, MUCH AGAINST HER WISHES, SHE TEARFULLY SAID GOODBYE TO HARETON AND LEFT WUTHERING HEIGHTS...

EDGAR AND CATHY LIVED HAPPILY AT THRUSHCROSS GRANGE FOR THE NEXT SIX MONTHS, EACH SHOWING THE UTMOST RESPECT FOR AND DEVOTION TO THE OTHER. THEN, ON A MELLOW EVENING IN SEPTEMBER, CAME A BREAK IN THEIR PLACID EXISTENCE...

ELLEN WAS COMING FROM THE GARDEN WITH A HEAVY BASKET OF APPLES SHE HAD BEEN GATHERING...

SUDDENLY, AS SHE STOPPED TO REST BY THE KITCHEN DOOR...

I HAVE WAITED HERE AN HOUR... I DARED NOT ENTER! LOOK, I'M NOT A STRANGER!

WHAT! YOU COME BACK? IS IT REALLY...

YES, HEATHCLIFF! ARE THEY AT HOME...WHERE IS SHE? I MUST HAVE ONE WORD WITH YOUR MISTRESS! TELL HER SOME PERSON FROM GIMMERTON DESIRES TO SEE HER!

HOW WILL SHE TAKE IT? IT WILL PUT HER OUT OF HER HEAD... AND, YOU ARE HEATHCLIFF, BUT ALTERED. I HARDLY RECOGNISED YOU.

GO AND CARRY MY MESSAGE. I CANNOT REST TILL YOU DO.

ELLEN SOON ENTERED THE PARLOUR...

A PERSON FROM GIMMERTON WISHES TO SEE YOU, MA'AM.

WISHES TO SEE ME? WELL, CLOSE THE CURTAINS, NELLY, AND BRING UP TEA! I'LL BE BACK DIRECTLY!

A MOMENT LATER...

OH, EDGAR, EDGAR!

OH, EDGAR, DARLING... HEATHCLIFF'S COME BACK... HE IS!

WELL, WELL, DON'T STRANGLE ME FOR THAT! HE NEVER STRUCK ME AS A MARVELOUS TREASURE. THERE IS NO NEED TO BE FRANTIC.

I KNOW YOU DIDN'T LIKE HIM, YET FOR MY SAKE YOU MUST BE FRIENDS NOW! SHALL I TELL HIM TO COME UP?

ELLEN WILL FETCH HIM... AND CATHERINE, TRY TO BE GLAD WITHOUT BEING ABSURD! THE WHOLE HOUSEHOLD NEED NOT WITNESS THE SIGHT OF YOUR WELCOMING A RUNAWAY SERVANT AS A BROTHER.

A FEW MOMENTS LATER, AFTER AN AWKWARD EXCHANGE OF GREETINGS...

SIT DOWN, SIR. OF COURSE, I AM HAPPY TO SEE YOU... IF IT PLEASES MRS. LINTON.

CRUEL HEATHCLIFF, YOU DO NOT DESERVE THIS WELCOME. TO BE ABSENT AND SILENT FOR SO LONG, AND NEVER TO THINK OF ME!

A LITTLE MORE THAN YOU HAVE THOUGHT OF ME. I'VE FOUGHT THROUGH A BITTER LIFE SINCE I LAST HEARD YOUR VOICE.

CATHERINE, UNLESS WE ARE TO HAVE COLD TEA, PLEASE COME UP TO THE TABLE. MR. HEATHCLIFF WILL HAVE A LONG WALK WHEREVER HE MAY LODGE TONIGHT, AND I'M THIRSTY!

AN HOUR LATER...

ARE YOU GOING TO GIMMERTON?

NO, TO WUTHERING HEIGHTS. MR. EARNSHAW INVITED ME WHEN I CALLED THIS MORNING.

WHEN HEATHCLIFF LEFT, ELLEN PONDERED HIS LAST WORDS PAINFULLY...

MR. EARNSHAW INVITED *HIM*... AND *HE* CALLED ON MR. EARNSHAW! I FEAR HE'S COME BACK TO WORK SOME MISCHIEF! WHY DID HE HAVE TO COME BACK?

IN THE DAYS THAT FOLLOWED, HEATHCLIFF WAS A FREQUENT VISITOR TO THE LINTON'S. ISABELLA LINTON, NOW A CHARMING YOUNG LADY OF EIGHTEEN, SUDDENLY SHOWED AN *IRRESISTIBLE* ATTRACTION TOWARD THE TOLERATED GUEST...

SHE GREW CROSS AND IRRITABLE WITH THE OTHER MEMBERS OF THE HOUSEHOLD. ONE EVENING...

IT'S YOUR HARSHNESS THAT MAKES ME UNHAPPY!

HOW CAN YOU SAY I AM HARSH? WHEN HAVE I BEEN HARSH?

YESTERDAY, IN OUR WALK ALONG THE MOOR! YOU TOLD ME TO RAMBLE WHERE I PLEASED, WHILE YOU SAUNTERED ON WITH MR. HEATHCLIFF!

AND THAT'S YOUR NOTION OF HARSHNESS? WHY, YOU SILLY CHILD... I MERELY THOUGHT THAT MR. HEATHCLIFF'S TALK WOULD HAVE NOTHING ENTERTAINING FOR YOUR EARS.

ISABELLA THEN CRIED OUT...

I LOVE HIM MORE THAN YOU EVER LOVED EDGAR! AND HE MIGHT LOVE ME IF YOU WOULD LET HIM!

I WOULDN'T BE YOU FOR A KINGDOM, THEN! YOU DON'T KNOW HEATHCLIFF LIKE I DO... HE IS A FIERCE, WOLFISH MAN! HE'D BE QUITE CAPABLE OF MARRYING YOU FOR YOUR FORTUNE AND EXPECTATIONS!

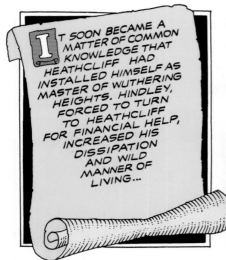

IT SOON BECAME A MATTER OF COMMON KNOWLEDGE THAT HEATHCLIFF HAD INSTALLED HIMSELF AS MASTER OF WUTHERING HEIGHTS. HINDLEY, FORCED TO TURN TO HEATHCLIFF FOR FINANCIAL HELP, INCREASED HIS DISSIPATION AND WILD MANNER OF LIVING...

ONE DAY, DEEPLY DISTURBED BY WHAT SHE HAD HEARD, ELLEN DECIDED TO PAY A VISIT TO WUTHERING HEIGHTS...

GOD BLESS YOU, DARLING! HARETON, IT'S NELLY, YOUR NURSE!

HE RETREATED AND PICKED UP A LARGE STONE, CURSING AND SWEARING AS HE DID...

HE DOESN'T RECOGNISE ME.

SHE OFFERED HIM AN ORANGE AND HE QUICKLY SNATCHED IT FROM HER HAND...

SHE OFFERED A SECOND ONE...

WHO HAS TAUGHT YOU THOSE FINE WORDS? THE CURATE?

BLAST THE CURATE AND YOU! GIVE ME THAT!

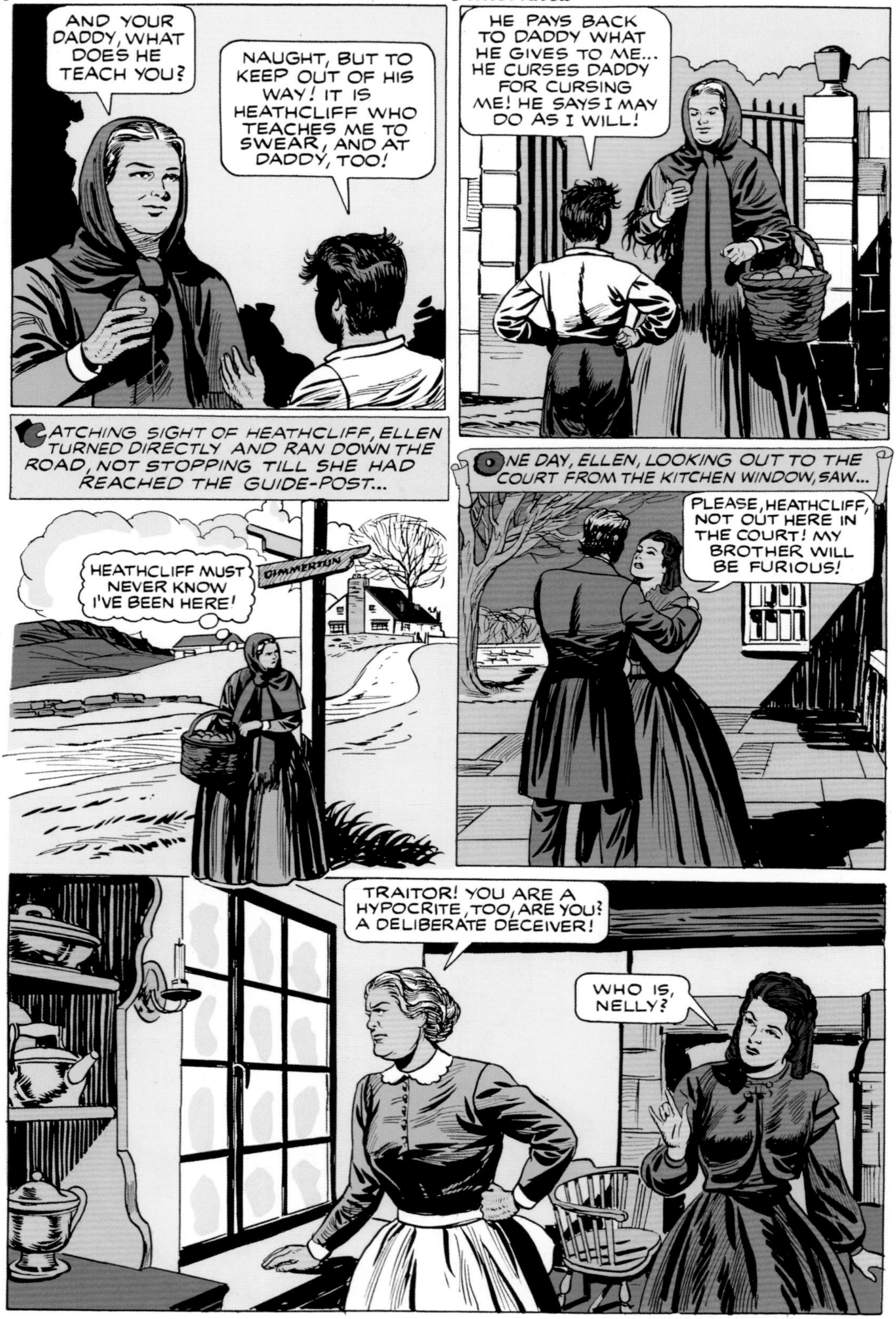
AND YOUR DADDY, WHAT DOES HE TEACH YOU?
NAUGHT, BUT TO KEEP OUT OF HIS WAY! IT IS HEATHCLIFF WHO TEACHES ME TO SWEAR, AND AT DADDY, TOO!
HE PAYS BACK TO DADDY WHAT HE GIVES TO ME... HE CURSES DADDY FOR CURSING ME! HE SAYS I MAY DO AS I WILL!
CATCHING SIGHT OF HEATHCLIFF, ELLEN TURNED DIRECTLY AND RAN DOWN THE ROAD, NOT STOPPING TILL SHE HAD REACHED THE GUIDE-POST...
HEATHCLIFF MUST NEVER KNOW I'VE BEEN HERE!
ONE DAY, ELLEN, LOOKING OUT TO THE COURT FROM THE KITCHEN WINDOW, SAW...
PLEASE, HEATHCLIFF, NOT OUT HERE IN THE COURT! MY BROTHER WILL BE FURIOUS!
TRAITOR! YOU ARE A HYPOCRITE, TOO, ARE YOU? A DELIBERATE DECEIVER!
WHO IS, NELLY?

YOUR WORTHLESS FRIEND, THE SNEAKING RASCAL YONDER! AH, HE'S CAUGHT A GLIMPSE OF US... HE'S COMING IN! I WONDER WILL HE HAVE THE HEART TO FIND A PLAUSIBLE EXCUSE FOR MAKING LOVE TO MISS!

A MOMENT LATER, HEATHCLIFF OPENED THE DOOR...

HEATHCLIFF, WHAT ARE YOU ABOUT, RAISING THIS STIR? I SAID YOU MUST LET ISABELLA ALONE! DO YOU WANT EDGAR TO FORBID YOUR COMING HERE?

HE'D BETTER NOT TRY! I'VE A RIGHT TO KISS HER, IF SHE CHOOSES, AND YOU'VE NO RIGHT TO OBJECT! I'M NOT YOUR HUSBAND... YOU NEEDN'T BE JEALOUS OF ME!

IF YOU LIKE ISABELLA, YOU SHALL MARRY HER.. BUT I KNOW YOU DON'T LIKE HER! ON THE CONTRARY, YOU TOLD ME YOURSELF YOU HATED HER!

I HAVE MY OWN GOOD REASONS FOR WHAT I DO, CATHY! IF I IMAGINED YOU REALLY WANTED ME TO MARRY HER, I'D CUT MY THROAT!

ELLEN LEFT THEM TO SEEK EDGAR, WHO WAS WONDERING WHAT KEPT CATHY BELOW SO LONG...

ELLEN, HAVE YOU SEEN YOUR MISTRESS?

YES, SHE'S IN THE KITCHEN. SHE'S SADLY PUT OUT BY MR. HEATHCLIFF'S BEHAVIOUR, AND, INDEED, I THINK IT TIME TO CALL OFF HIS VISITS HERE.

ELLEN THEN RELATED WHAT HAD HAPPENED...

THIS IS INSUFFERABLE! CALL ME TWO MEN OUT OF THE HALL, ELLEN. I HAVE HUMORED CATHERINE AND HER FRIEND ENOUGH!

A MOMENT LATER...

YOUR PRESENCE, SIR, IS A MORAL POISON, AND I GIVE YOU THREE MINUTES TO LEAVE THIS HOUSE, NEVER TO RETURN!

CATHY, THIS LAMB OF YOURS THREATENS LIKE A BULL! IT IS IN DANGER OF SPLITTING ITS SKULL AGAINST MY KNUCKLES!

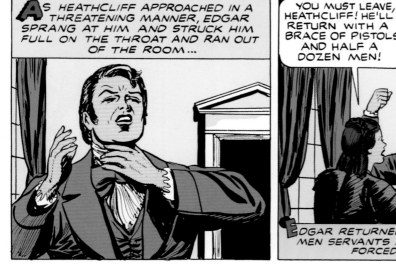

AS HEATHCLIFF APPROACHED IN A THREATENING MANNER, EDGAR SPRANG AT HIM AND STRUCK HIM FULL ON THE THROAT AND RAN OUT OF THE ROOM...

YOU MUST LEAVE, HEATHCLIFF! HE'LL RETURN WITH A BRACE OF PISTOLS AND HALF A DOZEN MEN!

I'LL CRUSH HIS RIBS IN LIKE A ROTTEN HAZEL NUT BEFORE I CROSS THE THRESHOLD! LET ME GET AT HIM!

EDGAR RETURNED WITH SOME OF THE MEN SERVANTS AND HEATHCLIFF WAS FORCED TO LEAVE...

FOR TWO DAYS, CATHY REMAINED SHUT UP IN HER ROOM, REFUSING TO ALLOW ELLEN TO ENTER WITH FOOD. EDGAR HAD AN INTERVIEW WITH ISABELLA, AND WARNED HER NOT TO ENCOURAGE THE RELATIONSHIP BETWEEN HERSELF AND HEATHCLIFF...

ON THE THIRD DAY, CATHY OPENED THE DOOR TO ELLEN...

IT'S ABOUT TIME YOU CAME TO YOUR SENSES, MISS. I'D THINK YOU'D SHOW SOME CONSIDERATION FOR MR. LINTON, AT LEAST!

WHAT IS THAT APATHETIC THING DOING? HAS HE FALLEN INTO A TRANCE OR IS HE DEAD?

HE'S TOLERABLY WELL, I THINK! HE'S CONTINUALLY AMONG HIS BOOKS, SINCE HE HAS NO OTHER SOCIETY.

AMONG HIS BOOKS! AND HERE I AM DYING! IS HE ACTUALLY SO INDIFFERENT FOR MY LIFE!

WHY, MA'AM, THE MASTER HAS NO IDEA YOU'RE IN DANGER. SURELY, HE DOESN'T FEAR THAT YOU'LL LET YOURSELF DIE OF HUNGER!

HOWEVER, CONTRARY TO ELLEN'S BELIEF, CATHY WAS DESPERATELY ILL. SHE WAS IN GRAVE DANGER OF LOSING HER MIND. THE COUNTY DOCTOR WAS CALLED AND KEPT WATCH OVER HER ALL THAT NIGHT...

THEN, ONE MORNING...

HOW IS SHE, DOCTOR?

SHE HAS PASSED THE CRISIS. BUT I WARN YOU TO KEEP HER FREE FROM ANY EXCITEMENT, OR I CANNOT BE RESPONSIBLE FOR THE CONSEQUENCES.

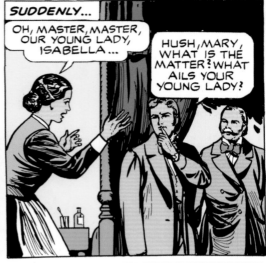

SUDDENLY...

OH, MASTER, MASTER, OUR YOUNG LADY, ISABELLA...

HUSH, MARY, WHAT IS THE MATTER? WHAT AILS YOUR YOUNG LADY?

SHE'S GONE, SHE'S GONE! HEATHCLIFF'S RUN OFF WITH HER!

THAT'S NOT TRUE! HOW HAS THE IDEA ENTERED YOUR HEAD? ELLEN, GO AND SEEK HER.

ELLEN RETURNED, CONFIRMING THE SERVANT'S STATEMENT...

ARE WE TO TRY ANY MEASURES FOR OVER-TAKING HER AND BRINGING HER BACK? HOW SHOULD WE DO?

SHE WENT OF HER OWN ACCORD. TROUBLE ME NO MORE ABOUT HER... HEREAFTER, SHE'S MY SISTER IN NAME ONLY.

ISABELLA LIVED AT WUTHERING HEIGHTS WHERE SHE WAS CRUELLY MISTREATED BY HEATHCLIFF.

ONE DAY, WHILE EDGAR WAS ABSENT, HEATHCLIFF PAID A SECRET VISIT TO CATHY AT THRUSHCROSS GRANGE. THE EXCITEMENT WAS TOO MUCH FOR HER, AND AT MIDNIGHT OF THE SAME DAY, SHE DIED, AFTER GIVING BIRTH TO A DAUGHTER...

POOR EDGAR... BUT HIS SORROW IS NOTHING TO THAT OF HEATHCLIFF'S WHEN HE LEARNS OF CATHY'S DEATH.

HEATHCLIFF, WHO HAD PROMISED TO RETURN THE NEXT DAY, WAS ACCOSTED BY ELLEN IN THE GARDEN. BEFORE SHE COULD SAY ANYTHING...

SHE'S DEAD! I'VE NOT WAITED FOR YOU, TO LEARN THAT! DON'T SNIVEL BEFORE ME... SHE WANTS NONE OF YOUR TEARS!

YES, SHE'S DEAD! GONE TO HEAVEN, I HOPE, WHERE WE MAY ALL JOIN HER IF WE TAKE DUE WARNING AND LEAVE OUR EVIL WAYS TO FIND GOOD!

HOW DID SHE DIE? DID SHE EVER MENTION ME?

QUIETLY AS A LAMB. HER LIFE CLOSED IN A GENTLE DREAM.

AT THAT, HE CRIED OUT IN ANGUISH...

CATHERINE EARNSHAW, MAY YOU NOT REST AS LONG AS I AM LIVING! BE WITH ME ALWAYS...TAKE MY FORM... DRIVE ME MAD! DON'T LEAVE ME IN THE ABYSS WHERE I CANNOT FIND YOU! I CANNOT LIVE WITHOUT MY LIFE! I CANNOT LIVE WITHOUT MY SOUL!

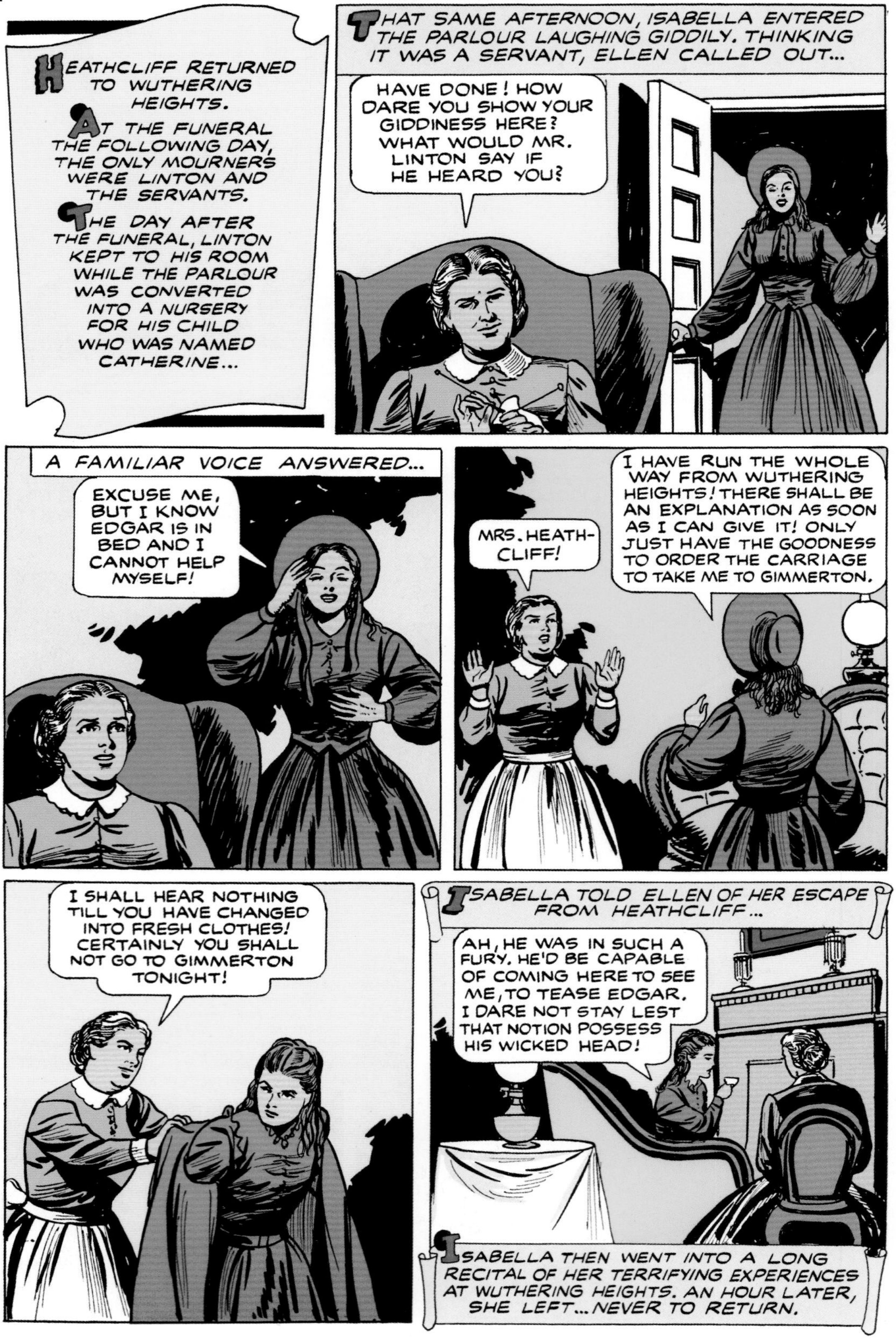
HEATHCLIFF RETURNED TO WUTHERING HEIGHTS.
AT THE FUNERAL THE FOLLOWING DAY, THE ONLY MOURNERS WERE LINTON AND THE SERVANTS.
THE DAY AFTER THE FUNERAL, LINTON KEPT TO HIS ROOM WHILE THE PARLOUR WAS CONVERTED INTO A NURSERY FOR HIS CHILD WHO WAS NAMED CATHERINE...
THAT SAME AFTERNOON, ISABELLA ENTERED THE PARLOUR LAUGHING GIDDILY. THINKING IT WAS A SERVANT, ELLEN CALLED OUT...
HAVE DONE! HOW DARE YOU SHOW YOUR GIDDINESS HERE? WHAT WOULD MR. LINTON SAY IF HE HEARD YOU?
A FAMILIAR VOICE ANSWERED...
EXCUSE ME, BUT I KNOW EDGAR IS IN BED AND I CANNOT HELP MYSELF!
MRS. HEATH-CLIFF!
I HAVE RUN THE WHOLE WAY FROM WUTHERING HEIGHTS! THERE SHALL BE AN EXPLANATION AS SOON AS I CAN GIVE IT! ONLY JUST HAVE THE GOODNESS TO ORDER THE CARRIAGE TO TAKE ME TO GIMMERTON.
I SHALL HEAR NOTHING TILL YOU HAVE CHANGED INTO FRESH CLOTHES! CERTAINLY YOU SHALL NOT GO TO GIMMERTON TONIGHT!
ISABELLA TOLD ELLEN OF HER ESCAPE FROM HEATHCLIFF...
AH, HE WAS IN SUCH A FURY. HE'D BE CAPABLE OF COMING HERE TO SEE ME, TO TEASE EDGAR. I DARE NOT STAY LEST THAT NOTION POSSESS HIS WICKED HEAD!
ISABELLA THEN WENT INTO A LONG RECITAL OF HER TERRIFYING EXPERIENCES AT WUTHERING HEIGHTS. AN HOUR LATER, SHE LEFT...NEVER TO RETURN.

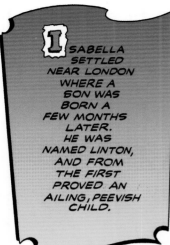

ISABELLA SETTLED NEAR LONDON WHERE A SON WAS BORN A FEW MONTHS LATER. HE WAS NAMED LINTON, AND FROM THE FIRST PROVED AN AILING, PEEVISH CHILD.

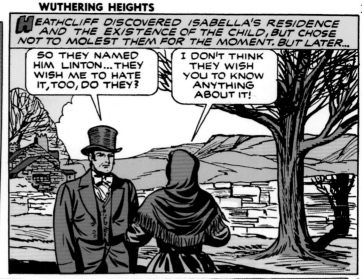

HEATHCLIFF DISCOVERED ISABELLA'S RESIDENCE AND THE EXISTENCE OF THE CHILD, BUT CHOSE NOT TO MOLEST THEM FOR THE MOMENT. BUT LATER...

SO THEY NAMED HIM LINTON...THEY WISH ME TO HATE IT, TOO, DO THEY?

I DON'T THINK THEY WISH YOU TO KNOW ANYTHING ABOUT IT!

BUT I'LL HAVE IT WHEN I WANT IT. THEY MAY RECKON ON THAT!

HINDLEY EARNSHAW DIED SOON AFTER, AND ELLEN WENT TO ATTEND THE FUNERAL...

THAT FOOL'S BODY SHOULD BE BURIED AT THE CROSS-ROADS, WITHOUT CEREMONY OF ANY KIND!

HE SEIZED HARETON AND LIFTED HIM ON THE TABLE...

THEY'LL NOT TAKE YOU BACK, MY BONNY LAD...YOU ARE MINE! AND WE'LL SEE IF ONE TREE WON'T GROW AS CROOKED AS ANOTHER, WITH THE SAME WIND TO TWIST IT!

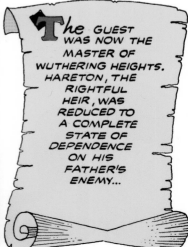

THE GUEST WAS NOW THE MASTER OF WUTHERING HEIGHTS. HARETON, THE RIGHTFUL HEIR, WAS REDUCED TO A COMPLETE STATE OF DEPENDENCE ON HIS FATHER'S ENEMY...

PEACE AND HAPPINESS MARKED THE NEXT TWELVE YEARS AT THRUSHCROSS GRANGE. DISTURBED ONE DAY BY THE NEWS ISABELLA HEATHCLIFF WAS DYING, EDGAR LEFT TO BE WITH HIS SISTER, LEAVING ELLEN ALONE WITH CATHY, NOW A YOUNG LADY, AND THE SERVANTS...

A FEW DAYS LATER, EDGAR RETURNED, ACCOMPANIED BY LINTON, ISABELLA'S SON...

THIS IS YOUR COUSIN CATHERINE, LINTON! SHE'S FOND OF YOU ALREADY! AND MIND YOU, DON'T GRIEVE HER BY CRYING TONIGHT!

LET ME GO TO BED, THEN; I'M SO TIRED!

OH, HE'LL DO VERY WELL...VERY WELL, IF WE CAN KEEP HIM!

AY, IF WE CAN KEEP HIM.

SEVERAL HOURS LATER, ELLEN'S WORST FEARS WERE REALISED...

WHAT BRINGS YOU FROM YOUR MASTER'S HOUSE, JOSEPH?

HEATHCLIFF HAS SENT ME FOR HIS LAD, AND I MAY NOT GO BACK WITHOUT HIM.

KNOWING IT WOULD BE USELESS TO KEEP LINTON AWAY FROM HIS RIGHTFUL FATHER, EDGAR RELUCTANTLY PROMISED TO SEND HIM OVER THE NEXT MORNING...

NEXT MORNING, HEATHCLIFF TOOK POSSESSION OF HIS RIGHTFUL HEIR...

I HOPE YOU'LL BE KIND TO THE BOY, HEATHCLIFF...OR YOU'LL NOT KEEP HIM LONG! AND REMEMBER, HE IS THE ONLY KIN YOU HAVE LEFT IN THE WORLD.

I'LL BE VERY KIND TO HIM, YOU NEEDN'T FEAR!

YES, NELL, MY SON IS PROSPECTIVE OWNER OF YOUR PLACE AND I SHOULD NOT WISH HIM TO DIE TILL I WAS CERTAIN OF BEING HIS SUCCESSOR! I DESPISE HIM FOR HIMSELF, AND I AM BITTERLY DISAPPOINTED WITH THE WHINING LITTLE WRETCH!

TIME WORE ON AT THE GRANGE IN A PLEASANT WAY TILL CATHERINE WAS SIXTEEN. ONE MORNING, SHE AND ELLEN DECIDED TO TAKE A RAMBLE ON THE EDGE OF THE MOORS...

WAIT FOR ME, CATHY, YOU'LL GET LOST!

WE'RE GETTING DANGEROUSLY CLOSE TO HEATHCLIFF'S PROPERTY, AND MR. LINTON HAS WARNED ME TO KEEP HER AWAY FROM THERE!

A MOMENT LATER...

WHAT ARE YOU DOING POACHING ON MY PROPERTY? AFTER GROUSE EGGS, I SUPPOSE?

I'VE NEITHER TAKEN NOR FOUND ANY! PAPA TOLD ME THERE WERE QUANTITIES OF EGGS HERE, AND I WISHED TO SEE THEM!

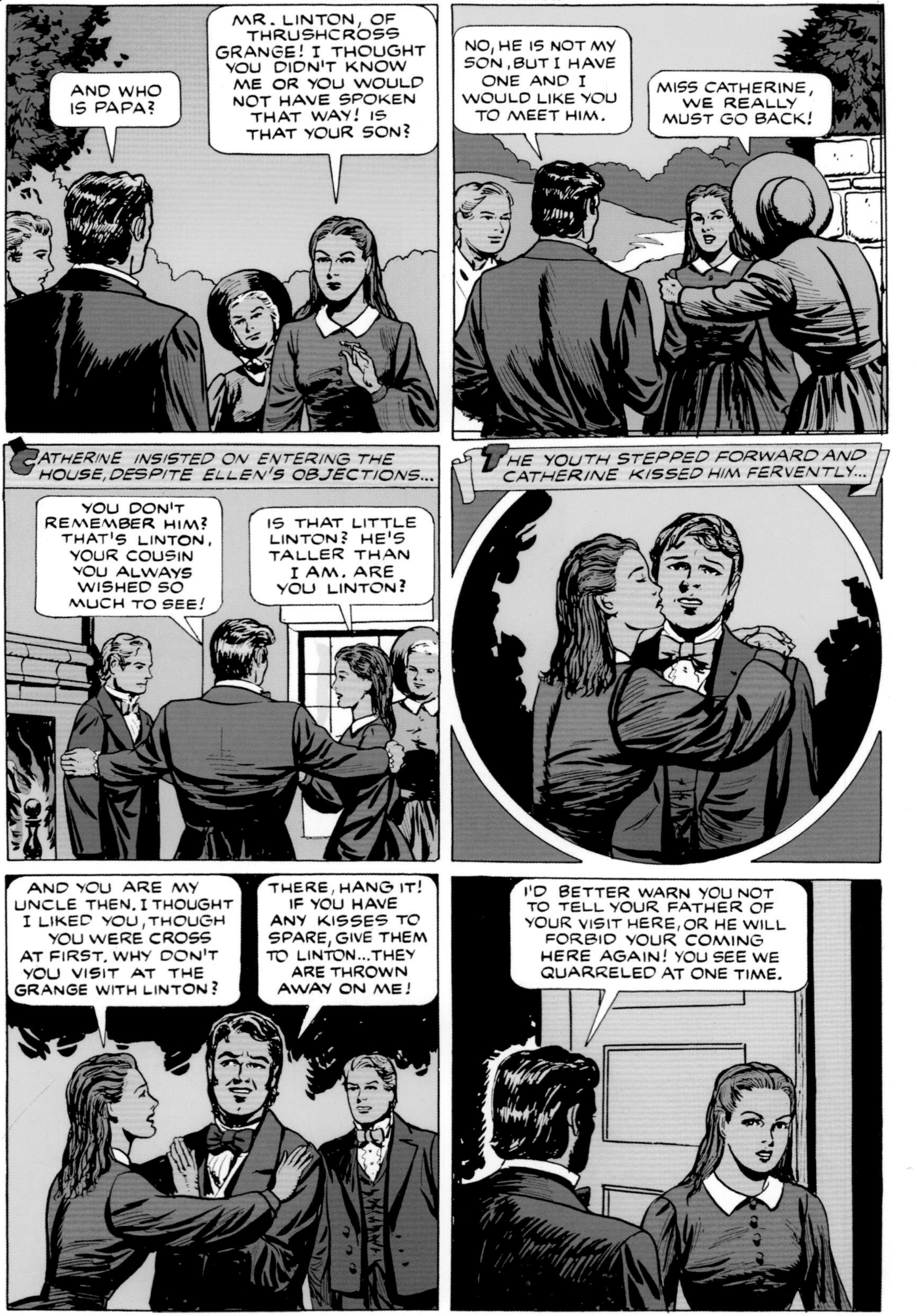
AND WHO IS PAPA?
MR. LINTON, OF THRUSHCROSS GRANGE! I THOUGHT YOU DIDN'T KNOW ME OR YOU WOULD NOT HAVE SPOKEN THAT WAY! IS THAT YOUR SON?
NO, HE IS NOT MY SON, BUT I HAVE ONE AND I WOULD LIKE YOU TO MEET HIM.
MISS CATHERINE, WE REALLY MUST GO BACK!
CATHERINE INSISTED ON ENTERING THE HOUSE, DESPITE ELLEN'S OBJECTIONS...
YOU DON'T REMEMBER HIM? THAT'S LINTON, YOUR COUSIN YOU ALWAYS WISHED SO MUCH TO SEE!
IS THAT LITTLE LINTON? HE'S TALLER THAN I AM. ARE YOU LINTON?
THE YOUTH STEPPED FORWARD AND CATHERINE KISSED HIM FERVENTLY...
AND YOU ARE MY UNCLE THEN. I THOUGHT I LIKED YOU, THOUGH YOU WERE CROSS AT FIRST. WHY DON'T YOU VISIT AT THE GRANGE WITH LINTON?
THERE, HANG IT! IF YOU HAVE ANY KISSES TO SPARE, GIVE THEM TO LINTON...THEY ARE THROWN AWAY ON ME!
I'D BETTER WARN YOU NOT TO TELL YOUR FATHER OF YOUR VISIT HERE, OR HE WILL FORBID YOUR COMING HERE AGAIN! YOU SEE WE QUARRELED AT ONE TIME.

IT WAS SEVERAL MONTHS LATER THAT CATHERINE COULD PERSUADE ELLEN TO TAKE HER THERE AGAIN...

NO, NO, DON'T KISS ME, MISS LINTON... IT TAKES MY BREATH AWAY!

I HEAR YOU ARE ILL... CAN I DO YOU ANY GOOD?

WHY DIDN'T YOU COME BEFORE? DO YOU KNOW THAT BRUTE HARETON LAUGHS AT ME? I HATE HIM... INDEED I HATE THEM ALL... THEY ARE ODIOUS BEINGS!

ABOUT THIS TIME, EDGAR LINTON BECAME VERY ILL AND WAS CONFINED TO HIS ROOM MOST OF THE TIME. CATHY CONTINUED HER SECRET VISITS TO WUTHERING HEIGHTS AND WAS SLOWLY FALLING INTO THE TRAP THAT HEATHCLIFF HAD SET FOR HER... THE BAIT BEING HIS WEAKLING SON, LINTON...

ONE DAY...

WELL, WE HAVE VISITORS AGAIN! HOW'S EVERYTHING AT THE GRANGE?

LOWERING HIS VOICE, HE SPOKE TO ELLEN...

I HEAR THAT EDGAR LINTON IS ON HIS DEATH-BED!

MY MASTER IS DYING. A SAD THING IT WILL BE FOR US ALL... BUT A BLESSING FOR HIM.

LINTON SEEMS DETERMINED TO UPSET MY PLANS. I'D THANK HIS UNCLE TO BE QUICK, AND GO BEFORE HIM! IS HE PRETTY LIVELY WITH MISS LINTON GENERALLY?

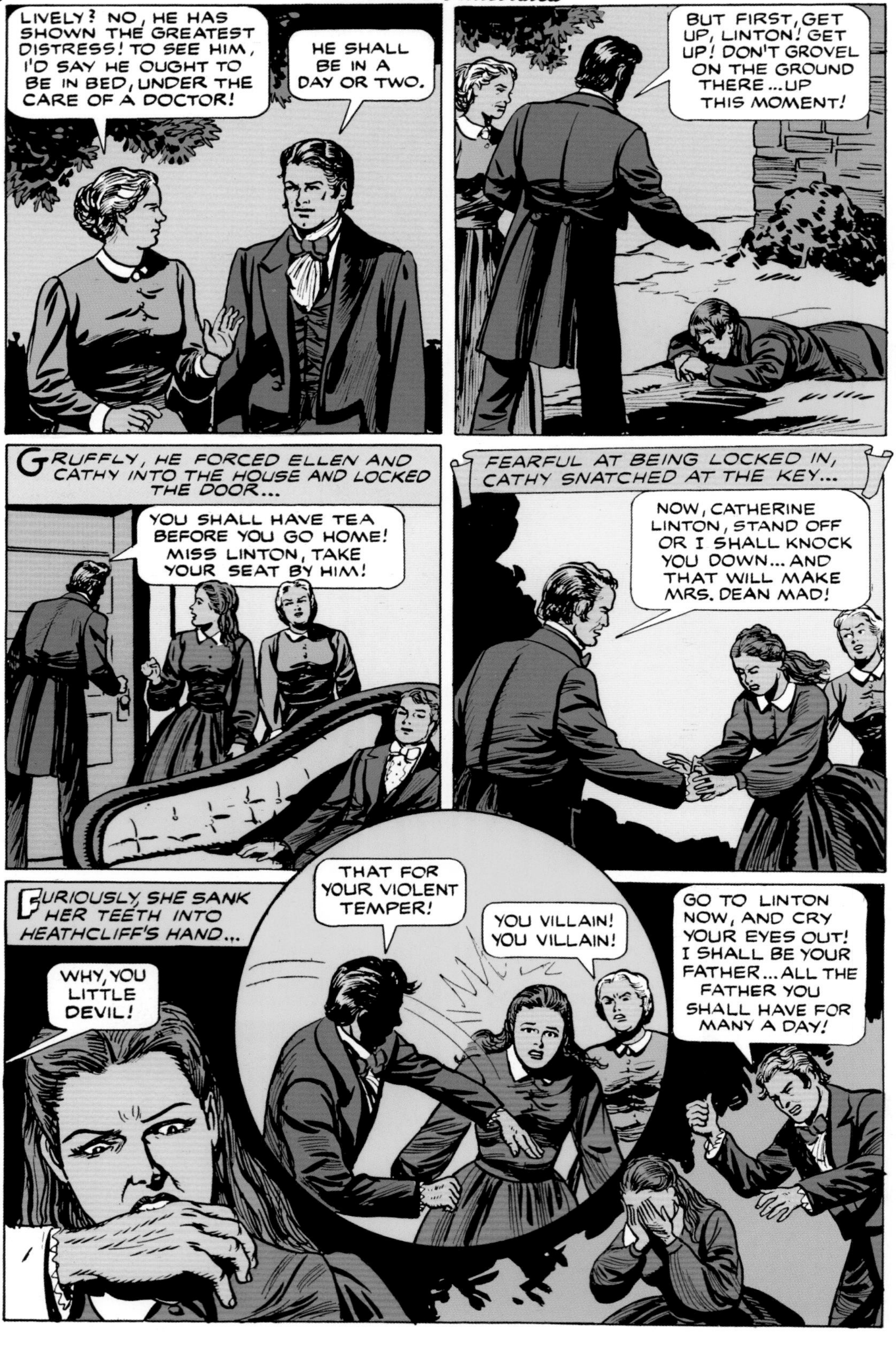
LIVELY? NO, HE HAS SHOWN THE GREATEST DISTRESS! TO SEE HIM, I'D SAY HE OUGHT TO BE IN BED, UNDER THE CARE OF A DOCTOR!
HE SHALL BE IN A DAY OR TWO.
BUT FIRST, GET UP, LINTON! GET UP! DON'T GROVEL ON THE GROUND THERE...UP THIS MOMENT!
GRUFFLY, HE FORCED ELLEN AND CATHY INTO THE HOUSE AND LOCKED THE DOOR...
YOU SHALL HAVE TEA BEFORE YOU GO HOME! MISS LINTON, TAKE YOUR SEAT BY HIM!
FEARFUL AT BEING LOCKED IN, CATHY SNATCHED AT THE KEY...
NOW, CATHERINE LINTON, STAND OFF OR I SHALL KNOCK YOU DOWN...AND THAT WILL MAKE MRS. DEAN MAD!
FURIOUSLY, SHE SANK HER TEETH INTO HEATHCLIFF'S HAND...
WHY, YOU LITTLE DEVIL!
THAT FOR YOUR VIOLENT TEMPER!
YOU VILLAIN! YOU VILLAIN!
GO TO LINTON NOW, AND CRY YOUR EYES OUT! I SHALL BE YOUR FATHER...ALL THE FATHER YOU SHALL HAVE FOR MANY A DAY!

ELLEN WAS RELEASED AFTER BEING HELD CAPTIVE FOUR DAYS AND WENT DIRECTLY TO HER MASTER'S ROOM. SHE RELATED HER EXPERIENCE AT WUTHERING HEIGHTS...

MY POOR BABY! THAT MONSTER IS PLOTTING TO SECURE MY PERSONAL PROPERTY THROUGH HER MARRIAGE TO LINTON! YOU MUST SEND FOR MY ATTORNEY TO CHANGE MY WILL!

ELLEN LOST NO TIME IN CARRYING OUT HIS INSTRUCTIONS...

SEND FOR MR. GREEN, THE ATTORNEY, AT ONCE... AND A HALF DOZEN OF THE MEN TO BRING MISS CATHERINE BACK!

LATE THE SAME AFTERNOON...

ELLEN, ELLEN, IS PAPA STILL ALIVE?

CATHERINE, IS IT REALLY YOU?

A MOMENT LATER...

I... AM... GOING TO HER! AND YOU, DARLING CHILD... SHALL COME TO US...

EDGAR DIED PEACEFULLY IN CATHERINE'S ARMS, THWARTED IN HIS PLAN TO CHANGE THE WILL...

LATER...

I'M GLAD FATHER DIED WITHOUT LEARNING THAT I'M MARRIED TO THE SON OF HIS BITTEREST ENEMY.

THEN HE DID CARRY OUT HIS THREAT. THE MONSTER WILL NOW LAY CLAIM TO YOU AS HIS OWN AND FORCE YOU TO LIVE WITH HIM AT WUTHERING HEIGHTS!

I'M RESIGNED TO IT NELLY. LINTON IS ALL I HAVE NOW.

THE FOLLOWING NIGHT...

I'D LIKE NOTHING BETTER THAN TO HAVE LINTON COME AND LIVE WITH US! I'D NEVER BE HAPPY LIVING HERE WITHOUT YOU!

NOTHING COULD PLEASE ME BETTER, ELLEN, BUT I'M AFRAID IT'S TOO MUCH TO HOPE FOR!

SUDDENLY...

THAT DEVIL HEATHCLIFF IS COMING IN THROUGH THE COURT. SHALL I FASTEN THE DOOR IN HIS FACE?

YOU SPEAK TO HIM, NELLY! I HAVE NO DESIRE TO SEE HIM.

STOP! NO MORE RUNNING AWAY! I'VE COME TO FETCH YOU HOME!

LINTON NEEDS YOU! HE WAKES AND SHRIEKS DURING THE NIGHT AND CALLS YOU TO PROTECT HIM FROM ME! HE'S YOUR CONCERN NOW!

WHY NOT LET CATHERINE CONTINUE HERE AND SEND MASTER LINTON TO HER? AS YOU HATE THEM BOTH, YOU WON'T MISS THEM.

I'M SEEKING A TENANT FOR THE GRANGE. MAKE HASTE...AND DON'T OBLIGE ME TO COMPEL YOU!

THEY LEFT, LEAVING ELLEN TO CARE FOR THRUSHCROSS GRANGE...

UPON HER ARRIVAL AT THE HEIGHTS, CATHERINE WENT DIRECTLY TO LINTON'S ROOM. A MOMENT LATER, SHE CAME RUNNING DOWN THE STAIRS, CRYING FRANTICALLY...

LINTON IS VERY ILL, HEATHCLIFF... YOU MUST SEND FOR A DOCTOR AT ONCE!

WE KNOW THAT! BUT HIS LIFE ISN'T WORTH A FARTHING, AND I WON'T SPEND A FARTHING ON HIM!

CATHERINE SPENT THE NEXT FEW DAYS NURSING HER DYING HUSBAND. THEN ONE NIGHT...

ZILLAH! TELL MR. HEATHCLIFF HIS SON IS DYING!

MERCY ME!

IN A FEW MINUTES, HE CAME INTO THE ROOM AND FOUND CATHERINE SEATED BY THE BED...

NOW, CATHERINE, HOW DO YOU FEEL?

HE'S SAFE, AND I'M FREE! I SHOULD FEEL WELL, BUT YOU'VE LEFT ME SO LONG TO STRUGGLE AGAINST DEATH ALONE, THAT I FEEL AND SEE ONLY DEATH!

SOME TIME LATER, ELLEN WAS SUMMONED TO WUTHERING HEIGHTS..AND OBEYED JOYFULLY FOR CATHERINE'S SAKE...

YOU SENT FOR ME?

YES, I'M TIRED OF CATHERINE. YOU'LL FIND HER IN THE KITCHEN!

NELLY, IT'S GOOD TO SEE YOU!

AND YOU, CATHY! YOU'RE LOOKING BADLY, MY CHILD!

CATHY POINTED TO HARETON...

NOT QUITE AS BADLY AS HE! LOOK, HE TWITCHES HIS NOSE LIKE MY DOG, JUNO, TWITCHES HERS.

MR. HARETON WILL TELL THE MASTER TO SEND YOU UPSTAIRS IF YOU DON'T BEHAVE!

DESPITE HER APPARENT CONTEMPT FOR HER COUSIN, CATHERINE REPEATEDLY MADE ATTEMPTS TO MAKE FRIENDS WITH HIM...

YOU SHOULD BE FRIENDS WITH CATHERINE, HARETON, SINCE SHE REPENTS HER SAUCINESS. IT WOULD MAKE YOU ANOTHER MAN TO HAVE HER FOR A COMPANION.

WHEN SHE HATES ME! NAY, I'LL NOT SEEK HER GOOD-WILL IF IT WOULD MAKE ME KING!

IT IS NOT I WHO HATE YOU; IT IS YOU WHO HATE ME! YOU HATE ME EVEN MORE THAN MR. HEATH-CLIFF!

WHY HAVE I ANGERED HIM, THEN, BY TAKING YOUR PART A HUNDRED TIMES? AND THAT, WHEN YOU DESPISED AND SNEERED AT ME?

I DIDN'T KNOW YOU TOOK MY PART, AND I WAS MISERABLE AND BITTER AT EVERYBODY... BUT NOW, I THANK YOU AND BEG YOUR FORGIVENESS.

CATHERINE BESTOWED A GENTLE KISS ON HIS CHEEK AND THEY WERE FAST FRIENDS THEREAFTER...

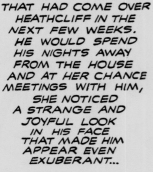

IT WAS ELLEN WHO FIRST NOTICED THE CHANGE THAT HAD COME OVER HEATHCLIFF IN THE NEXT FEW WEEKS. HE WOULD SPEND HIS NIGHTS AWAY FROM THE HOUSE AND AT HER CHANCE MEETINGS WITH HIM, SHE NOTICED A STRANGE AND JOYFUL LOOK IN HIS FACE THAT MADE HIM APPEAR EVEN EXUBERANT...

ONE MORNING...

WILL YOU HAVE SOME BREAKFAST? YOU MUST BE HUNGRY RAMBLING ABOUT ALL NIGHT.

NO, I'M NOT HUNGRY... JUST GO ABOUT YOUR WORK AND LET ME ALONE!

HE'LL WORK HIMSELF INTO A FIT OF ILLNESS! I CANNOT CONCEIVE WHAT HE HAS BEEN DOING!

HE LEFT HIS FOOD UNTOUCHED ALL DAY, AND THAT EVENING, ELLEN SPOKE TO HIM AGAIN...

HAVE YOU ANY GOOD NEWS, MR. HEATHCLIFF? YOU LOOK UNCOMMONLY ANIMATED.

WHERE SHOULD GOOD NEWS COME FROM FOR ME? TODAY, I AM WITHIN SIGHT OF MY HEAVEN! I HAVE MY EYES WITHIN SIGHT OF IT!

AND NOW YOU'D BETTER GO! I CAN'T HAVE YOU PRYING INTO MY AFFAIRS!

IT RAINED ALL THAT NIGHT, AND NEXT MORNING, ELLEN CHANCED TO LOOK UP AT HEATHCLIFF'S WIDE-OPEN WINDOWS...

HE CANNOT BE IN BED...THOSE SHOWERS WOULD DRENCH HIM THROUGH! I'LL GO UP AND SEE FOR MYSELF!

ENTERING THE ROOM TO CLOSE THE WINDOWS, SHE RECEIVED A SEVERE SHOCK...

GOOD HEAVENS!

STARK DEAD!

SEIZED WITH A FIT OF TREMBLING, SHE CALLED OUT FOR JOSEPH...

JOSEPH, COME QUICKLY! THE MASTER'S DEAD!

JOSEPH SHUFFLED QUIETLY INTO THE ROOM...

THE DEVIL'S CARRIED OFF HIS SOUL, AND HE MAY HAVE HIS CARCASS INTO THE BARGAIN! WHAT A WICKED ONE HE LOOKS, GRINNING AT DEATH!

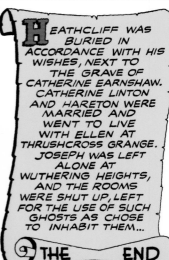

HEATHCLIFF WAS BURIED IN ACCORDANCE WITH HIS WISHES, NEXT TO THE GRAVE OF CATHERINE EARNSHAW. CATHERINE LINTON AND HARETON WERE MARRIED AND WENT TO LIVE WITH ELLEN AT THRUSHCROSS GRANGE. JOSEPH WAS LEFT ALONE AT WUTHERING HEIGHTS, AND THE ROOMS WERE SHUT UP, LEFT FOR THE USE OF SUCH GHOSTS AS CHOSE TO INHABIT THEM...

THE END

How Clear She Shines

by Emily Brontë

How clear she shines! How quietly
I lie beneath her guardian light;
While heaven and earth are whispering me,
"To morrow, wake, but dream to-night."
Yes, Fancy, come, my Fairy love!
These throbbing temples softly kiss;
And bend my lonely couch above,
And bring me rest, and bring me bliss.

The world is going; dark world, adieu!
Grim world, conceal thee till the day;
The heart thou canst not all subdue
Must still resist, if thou delay!

Thy love I will not, will not share;
Thy hatred only wakes a smile;
Thy griefs may wound—thy wrongs may tear,
But, oh, thy lies shall ne'er beguile!
While gazing on the stars that glow
Above me, in that stormless sea,
I long to hope that all the woe
Creation knows, is held in thee!

And this shall be my dream to-night;
I'll think the heaven of glorious spheres
Is rolling on its course of light
In endless bliss, through endless years;
I'll think, there's not one world above,
Far as these straining eyes can see,
Where Wisdom ever laughed at Love,
Or Virtue crouched to Infamy;

Where, writhing 'neath the strokes of Fate,
The mangled wretch was forced to smile;
To match his patience 'gainst her hate,
His heart rebellious all the while.
Where Pleasure still will lead to wrong,
And helpless Reason warn in vain;
And Truth is weak, and Treachery strong;
And Joy the surest path to Pain;
And Peace, the lethargy of Grief;
And Hope, a phantom of the soul;
And life, a labour, void and brief;
And Death, the despot of the whole!

(1843)

Themes

The British class system

The novel is set at a time when capitalism and industrialisation are changing not only the economy but also the traditional social structure and the relationship of the classes.

As members of the 'gentry', the Earnshaws and the Lintons occupy a somewhat precarious place within the hierarchy of late eighteenth- and early nineteenth-century British society. At the top of British society was royalty, followed by the aristocracy, then by the gentry, and then by the lower classes, who made up the vast majority of the population. Although the gentry, or upper middle class, possessed servants and often large estates, they held a nonetheless fragile social position. The social status of aristocrats was a formal and settled matter, because they usually had official titles. Members of the gentry, however, rarely held titles, and their status was therefore subject to change. A man might see himself as a gentleman but find that his neighbours or erstwhile peers did not share this view. A discussion of whether or not a man was really a gentleman would consider such questions as how much land he owned, how many tenants and servants he had, how he spoke, whether he kept horses and a carriage, and whether his money came from land or "trade"— true gentlemen scorned commercial activities.

Considerations of class status often crucially inform the characters' motivations in *Wuthering Heights*. Catherine's decision to marry Edgar so that she will be "the greatest woman of the neighbourhood" is only one of many examples. The Lintons are relatively secure in their status, but nonetheless are at great pains to prove this through their possessions, dress and manners. The Earnshaws, on the other hand, reside on much shakier ground socially. They do not have a carriage, they have less land, and their house, as Lockwood remarks, resembles that of a "homely, northern farmer" and not that of a gentleman. The shifting nature of social

Cont'd

status is demonstrated most strikingly in Heathcliff's trajectory from homeless orphaned waif to young gentleman-by-adoption to common labourer to gentleman again (although the status-conscious Lockwood remarks that Heathcliff is only a gentleman in "dress and manners").

———————————∞———————————

The Brontë family themselves held an unusual position in society, in that they had more income than the majority of people in Haworth, but not enough wealth to socialise among the upper middle classes.

Patrick Brontë's income of about £200 per year was twenty times more than that of the average domestic servant, but the Brontë family were poor in comparison with landowners or wealthy aristocrats whose income might be more than £10,000 or even £20,000 per year.

The Parsonage was one of the largest houses in Haworth, but again small in comparison with the homes of clergymen in more wealthy areas of Britain.

In spite of their relative wealth, the Brontës could not afford to keep a carriage, nor travel widely, nor dress and furnish their home in the same way that the upper classes and wealthy manufacturers of Yorkshire did.

That the sisters all had to take paid employment was enough to relegate them in class terms.

Brontë Country

The Brontë Country is a name given to an area of the south Pennine hills, west of Leeds/Bradford in West Yorkshire, England. The name is taken from those famous inhabitants – the Brontë sisters, who wrote the literary classics *Jane Eyre* (Charlotte Brontë), *Wuthering Heights* (Emily Brontë), and *The Tenant of Wildfell Hall* (Anne Brontë) whilst living in the area.

Unlike the limestone valleys of the Yorkshire Dales which begin further to the north, the geology in Brontë Country is predominantly of Millstone Grit, a dark sandstone which lends the crags and scenery here an air of bleakness and desolation. The area includes the village of Haworth, where the Brontë sisters lived, and where the Brontë Parsonage Museum is located today.

Haworth, located 800 feet high in the Pennines, was a crowded industrial township during the Brontë period. The population increased by 118 percent between 1801 and 1851 to 3,365. There were no sewers and the water supply was both polluted and inadequate, contributing to a high mortality rate.

There were 1,344 burials in the church yard between 1840 and 1850 and the average age at death was 25 years; 41 percent of children died before reaching their sixth birthday.

Though tourists are often told that Top Withens, a ruined farmhouse near the Haworth Parsonage (Brontë Parsonage Museum), is the model for Wuthering Heights, it seems more likely that the now demolished High Sunderland Hall, near Halifax was a partial model for the building. This Gothic edifice, near Law Hill, where Emily worked briefly as a schoolmistress in 1838, had grotesque embellishments of griffins and misshapen nude men similar to those described by Lockwood of *Wuthering Heights* in chapter one of the novel:

"Before passing the threshold, I paused to admire a quantity of grotesque carving lavished over the front, and especially about the

Cont'd

principal door, above which, among a wilderness of crumbling griffins and shameless little boys, I detected the date '1500'".

The originals of Thrushcross Grange have been traditionally connected to Ponden Hall near Haworth (although it is far too small) and, more likely, Shibden Hall, near Halifax A feud centered around Walterclough Hall is also said to have been one inspiration for the story.

Other places of interest from the Brontë sisters' novels include Oakwell Hall (Fieldhead in Charlotte's *Shirley*), Red House (Briarmains in *Shirley*), Gawthorpe Hall and Wycoller Hall (Ferndean Manor in *Jane Eyre*).

The Brontë Trail

There is a nature trail known as the Brontë Trail starting from Haworth and running over the moors to the waterfall. Continuing on, Top Withens can be reached on the same walk. The Brontë Parsonage Museum at Haworth is maintained by the Brontë Society in honour of the famed sisters — Charlotte, Emily and Anne — and It is popular with those seeking to find the source of the sisters' inspiration. It is of particular interest as the Brontës spent most of their lives here and wrote their famous novels in these rooms and surroundings.

The Brontë Society is open to everyone to join. It is one of the oldest literary societies in the English speaking world, and is also a registered charity. The Society welcomes new members to support the preservation of the museum and library collections for future generations and to tell the story of the Brontës' lives and works.

The Brontë Family Tree and List of Works

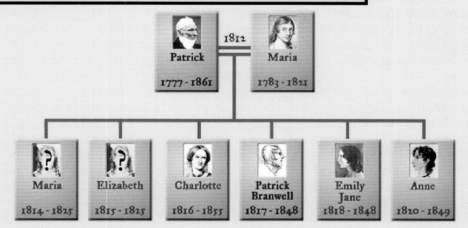

Charlotte Brontë
Jane Eyre (1846)
Villette (1853)
Shirley (1849)
The Professor (1857)
High Life in Verdopolis

Juvenilia: 1829-1835

Emily Brontë
Wuthering Heights (1847)

Anne Brontë
Agnes Grey (1847)
The Tenant of Wildfell Hall (1848)

Branwell Brontë
The Works of Patrick Branwell Brontë: An Edition (Vol. 1)

Cont'd

The three sisters also compiled a number of their poems into a collection of poetry called *Poems by Currer, Ellis, and Acton Bell*. Currer, Ellis, and Acton were the aliases used by the sisters to disguise their feminine identities.

Best Poems of the Brontë Sisters
Brontë: Poems (Emily)
The Complete Poems (Emily)
Selected Poems (Charlotte, Emily, Anne, and Branwell)

Charlotte began several novels, but never finished them. There is a book called *Unfinished Novels* that includes these fragments. The book contains: *The Story of Willie Ellin, Ashworth, The Moores,* and *Emma.*

Emily Jane Brontë (1818-1848)

Emily Jane Brontë was born in Thornton, England, August, 1818. Her father was Patrick Brontë (born Brunty). His wife died of cancer in 1821, leaving him with six children. Of the six, Charlotte, Emily and Anne were destined to become famous for their extraordinary literary gifts.

The family moved to Haworth just three months after Anne's birth, where Patrick remained as rector until his death in 1861.

Legend has grown around the figure of Emily Brontë, and criticism has confused her character with those she created. We now do not have an entirely clear picture of her life, save for what was written of her by her sister, Charlotte.

The sisters were educated at home, except for one year, which Maria, Elizabeth, Charlotte and Emily spent in the Clergy Daughter's School at Cowan's Bridge.

Early in 1842, Emily accompanied Charlotte on a trip to Brussels where they became pupils in the Pensionatt Heger. Their talent in English brought them to the attention of their headmaster, Constantin Heger, who guided them in their rapid acquisition of a mastery of the language. Their studies were, however, cut short after eight months by the death of an aunt, causing them to return to England. While Charlotte had been happy in Brussels, Emily had pined for the wild moorland air of her home.

Their aunt had bequeathed to them a sum which carried with it a certain independence, and the sisters began taking pupils at their father's house.

Emily's poems (she alone of the sisters possessed a true poetic gift) reveal the most about her mind and heart. From them, we learn of her stoicism and of her passion for the moors, which almost amounted to "nature worship".

Emily is great alike as a novelist and as a poet. Her *Old Stoic* and *Last Lives* were among the finest achievements of poetry that any woman has given to English literature. *Wuthering Heights* stands alone as a monument of her intensity. It was a thing apart: passionately sincere, unforgettable, haunting in its grimness, its grey melancholy. It is essential to realise the early Victorian atmosphere in which Emily and Charlotte Brontë wrote their novels if the greatest of their achievement is to be realised. Their world was built up in their own imagination, and it is this which makes its truth and its universal appeal.

Emily died on 9th December 1848, at the young age of thirty. With her death, perhaps the greatest of the Brontës passed away.